WARNING!

Scaredy Squirrel insists that
everyone check under their
beds before reading this book.

To Joe, who dreams about getting a little more sleep

Text and illustrations © 2009 Mélanie Watt

This edition is only available for distribution through the school market by Scholastic Book Fairs and Scholastic Canada, Ltd.

ISBN 978-1-55453-463-0

CM PA 10 0 9 8 7 6 5 4 3 2 1

Kids Can Press acknowledges the financial support of the Government of Ontario, through the Ontario Media Development Corporation's Ontario Book Initiative; the Ontario Arts Council; the Canada Council for the Arts; and the Government of Canada, through the BPIDP, for our publishing activity.

Published in Canada by
Kids Can Press Ltd.
25 Dockside Drive
Toronto, ON M5A 0B5

Published in the U.S. by
Kids Can Press Ltd.
2250 Military Road
Tonawanda, NY 14150

www.kidscanpress.com

The artwork in this book was rendered digitally in Photoshop.
The text is set in Potato Cut.

Edited by Tara Walker
Designed by Mélanie Watt and Karen Powers

The hardcover edition of this book is smyth sewn casebound.
The paperback edition of this book is limp sewn with a drawn-on cover.
Manufactured in Tseung Kwan O, NT Hong Kong, China, in 5/2010 by Paramount Printing Co. Ltd.

CM 09 0 9 8 7 6 5 4 3

LIBRARY AND ARCHIVES CANADA CATALOGUING IN PUBLICATION

Watt, Mélanie, 1975–
    Scaredy Squirrel at night / written and illustrated by Mélanie Watt.

ISBN 978-1-55453-288-9

I. Title.

PS8645.A884S2826 2009   jC813'.6   C2008-904793-1

Kids Can Press is a **Corus**™ Entertainment company

Scaredy Squirrel

at night

by Mélanie Watt

KIDS CAN PRESS

Scaredy Squirrel never sleeps.
He'd rather stay awake than risk having
a bad dream in the middle of the night.

A few creatures Scaredy Squirrel is afraid could appear in a bad dream:

dragons

fairies

ghosts

unicorns

vampire bats

polka-dot monsters

So he's very determined to stay awake
by keeping busy all through the night.

SCAREDY'S NIGHTTIME "TO DO" LIST

1. Count stars
(should keep you occupied for a while)

2. Play Cymbals
(loud, annoying noise is sure to keep you wide awake)

3. Take up scrapbooking
(keeps you well-organized and productive)

So night after night ...

after night ...

after night ...

Scaredy avoids sleeping.

BUT ...

SIDE EFFECTS OF SLEEPLESS NIGHTS MAY INCLUDE:

energy loss

forgetfulness

drowsiness

moodiness

poor reflexes

hallucinations

confusion ...

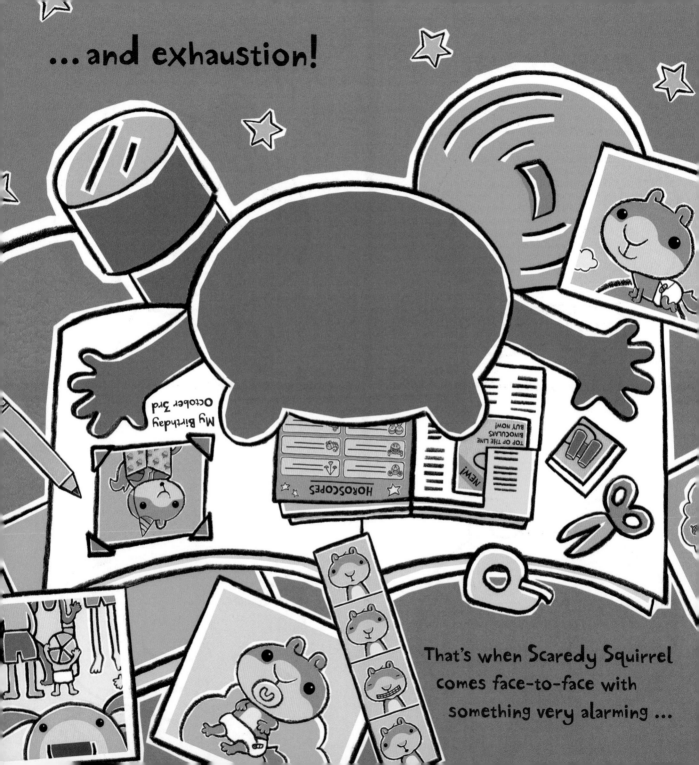

HOROSCOPES

FIND OUT WHAT THE STARS PREDICT FOR YOU!

 Aries (March 21–April 19)
You can climb mountains!

   Libra (Sept. 23– Oct. 22)
Get ready. At midnight all your dreams will come true!

 Taurus (April 20–May 20)
Take the bull by the horns!

 Scorpio (Oct. 23–Nov. 21)
Look out or you'll be stung!

 Gemini (May 21–June 21)
Two heads are always better than one!

 Sagittarius (Nov. 22–Dec. 21)
Aim for your goals!

 Cancer (June 22–July 22)
Claw your way to success!

Capricorn (Dec. 22–Jan. 19)
You're halfway there!

 Leo (July 23–Aug. 22)
You're the king of the jungle!

 Aquarius (Jan. 20–Feb. 18)
Go with the flow!

 Virgo (Aug. 23–Sept. 22)
Spread your wings and fly!

  Pisces (Feb. 19–March 20)
There are plenty of fish in the sea!

A few things Scaredy Squirrel needs to face his bad dreams:

spotlight

cupcakes

banana peels

fire extinguisher

safety cones

fan

teddy bear (decoy)

DO NOT DISTURB

sign

pillow and blanket

MOLASSES

molasses

BAD DREAM ACTION PLAN

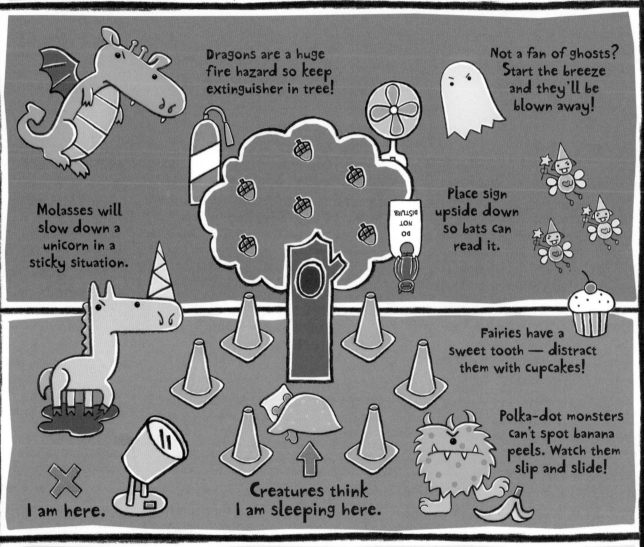

Dragons are a huge fire hazard so keep extinguisher in tree!

Not a fan of ghosts? Start the breeze and they'll be blown away!

Molasses will slow down a unicorn in a sticky situation.

Place sign upside down so bats can read it.

DO NOT DISTURB

Fairies have a sweet tooth — distract them with cupcakes!

Polka-dot monsters can't spot banana peels. Watch them slip and slide!

X I am here.

Creatures think I am sleeping here.

IMPORTANT: These creatures avoid light. Hide behind spotlight, switch it on at midnight and creatures will disappear! Remember, if all else fails, **PLAY DEAD** until sunrise.

So Scaredy Squirrel gets into position.
As he counts down to midnight, his bad
dreams seem to come true, one by one.

But when he turns on the spotlight ...

Hungry intruders appear!

This was **NOT** part of the Plan!

Scaredy Squirrel panics!

He steps in the molasses ...

He stumbles over a safety cone ...

PLEASE
CLEAN
UP!

He slips and slides
on a banana peel ...

MOLASSES

He lands on
the pillow ...

AND ...

8 hours later, Scaredy Squirrel finally wakes up.

BENEFITS OF A GOOD NIGHT'S SLEEP MAY INCLUDE:

energy gain

sharper memory

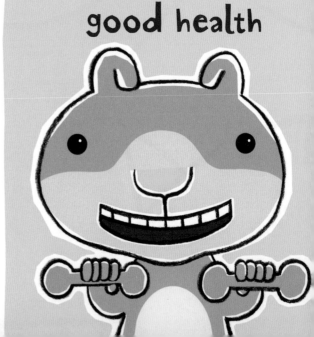

good health

happiness

better reflexes

peacefulness

cleverness ...

... and clear thinking!

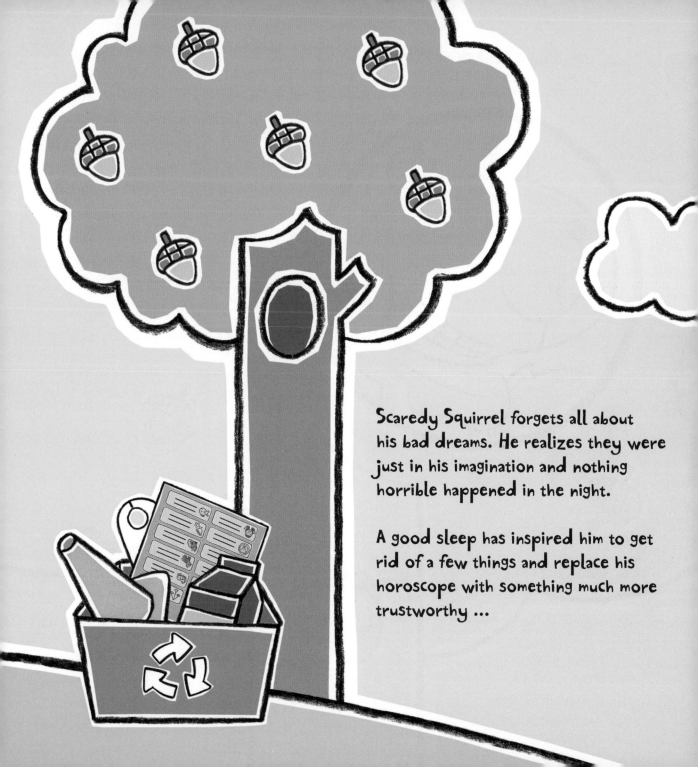

Scaredy Squirrel forgets all about his bad dreams. He realizes they were just in his imagination and nothing horrible happened in the night.

A good sleep has inspired him to get rid of a few things and replace his horoscope with something much more trustworthy ...